Lulu loves the Library

Anna McQuinn

Illustrated by Rosalind Beardshaw

ALANNA BOOKS

Lulu loves Tuesdays.
On Tuesdays, Lulu and her
mummy go to the library.

The library opens at nine o'clock
but Lulu is ready to go
long before that!

She puts all the books she borrowed
last week in her rucksack.

Her library card is also VERY important.

The library is not very
far away, so Lulu and
her mummy always walk there.

Lulu and her mummy give back
the books from last week. The librarian
buzzes them through her machine.

There's a special section in the library just for children.

It's really cool and nobody ever says, "shhh!"

Sometimes they even have singing.

Lulu knows all the words
AND the actions for
"Twinkle, Twinkle, Little Star."

Sometimes they have storytime.
Lulu loves that.

After storytime, Lulu chooses
her books. In the library,
she can have ANY book she wants.

Lulu likes stories with bears
and ANYTHING with shoes.
There are so many,
it takes ages to choose!

Mummy has some books, too.
The librarian buzzes them
through the machine,
then stamps the date inside.

Lulu must bring them
back in two weeks,
but she will probably be back
for more long before then!

Lulu and her mummy always go for
a coffee after visiting the library.
Mummy has a cappuccino
and Lulu has juice.

Whenever Lulu has been good, her mummy
lets her taste the froth – mmmmm!

Then it's time to go home again.

Every night, when Lulu is tucked up in bed, her mummy reads her a story.
Sometimes it's nice to read a new story...

**but sometimes an old favourite
is the best way to end the day.**

Dedicated with thanks to Rana, Malika, Noor, Angel, Zahra,
Hassan, Ashleigh, Shannon, Mathilde, Tabitha, Honor, Alejo,
Oscar, Benjamin, Max, Anastasia, Alexandro, Nawaal, Vita,
Philmon, Nahome, Nicholas, Matthew, Farah, Atifa, India,
Sabri, Caitlin, Katie, Anuska, Sol, Zak and all the 'regulars'
in the Sure Start Family Book Group in Acton Library.

To Zaynab and Milgo for helping with the research;
to Abir for not complaining all the mornings Sally woke
her up early to come to the Book Group,
and to Husain for sharing my cappuccino, AMcQ

To Philippa, with love, RB

First published in the United Kingdom in 2006
by Alanna Books
46 Chalvey Road East, Slough, Berkshire,
SL1 2LR, United Kingdom

ISBN 13: 978-0-9551998-0-6   ISBN 10: 0-9551998-0-8

Printed in China